D0678480

Subject to Change

Subject to Change

Poems by Marilyn L. Taylor

David Robert Books

© 2004 Marilyn L. Taylor

Published by David Robert Books
P.O. Box 541106
Cincinnati, OH 45254-1106

ISBN: 1932339035
LCCN: 2003105738

Typeset in ITC Cheltenham Book BT by WordTech
Communications LLC, Cincinnati, OH

Visit us on the web at www.davidrobertbooks.com

Poetry Editor: Kevin Walzer
Business Editor: Lori Jareo

Acknowledgments

With thanks to the editors of the following journals in which these poems first appeared:

The American Scholar: "Rondeau: Old Woman with Cat"
The Cream City Review: "After Twenty Years," "The Native"
Dogwood Journal: "Notes from the Good-Girl Chronicles, 1963"
The Formalist: "Reading the Obituaries," "Splitting"
Iris: "For Lucy, Who Came First"
Journal of the American Medical Association: "Another Thing I
      Ought to Be Doing"
The Ledge: "Dispatch from the Cold War, 1951," "Always
      Questions"
Passager: "Aunt Eudora's Harlequin Romance"
Poetry: "Summer Sapphics," "Poem for a 75th Birthday," "The
      Geniuses Among Us," "Subject to Change"
Smartish Pace: "Voice Mail for Wallace Stevens," "To a Cat Gone
      Blind in his 18th Summer"
Southern California Anthology: "Outside the Frame"
Wisconsin Poets Calendar, 2003: "Surveying the Damage"

Additionally, "The Aging Huntress Speaks to Her Reflection," "I
Miss You and I'm Drunk," and "The Agnostic's Villanelle" were the
winners of a literary award from *Passager,* and originally
appeared in that magazine.

"Explication of a True Story" was the winner of a literary award
from *The Ledge,* and originally appeared in that journal.

"On Learning, Late in Life, that Your Mother Was a Jew" was the
winner of a literary award from *GSU Review,* and originally
appeared in that journal.

"Notes from the Good-Girl Chronicles, 1963" was the winner of a literary award from *Dogwood*, and originally appeared in that journal.

The cover art is by Diane Knox. The author photograph is by Patrick Manning.

For Allen and Reed

Contents

I. MOODS
Summer Sapphics   3
For Lucy, Who Came First   4
Reading the Obituaries   5
Poem for a 75th Birthday   6
The Blue Water Buffalo   7
The Geniuses Among Us   8
Foreigner   9
Notes from the Good-Girl Chronicles, 1963   10

II. STATES OF MIND
Subject to Change   19
On Learning, Late in Life, that Your Mother Was a Jew 20
I Miss You and I'm Drunk   22
The Belgian Half   23
The Aging Huntress Speaks to Her Reflection   24
Always Questions   25
Explication of a True Story   26
Legacy   28
After Twenty Years   29
Women at Sixty   31
Rondeau: Old Woman with Cat   33
Father Goose   34

III. SCENES
Aunt Eudora's Harlequin Romance   37
Another Thing I Ought to Be Doing   38
The Native   39
Splitting   40
Inventing the Love Poets   41
Aunt Eudora in Paris   42

The Adulterer's Waltz   43
Surveying the Damage   44
Listening to Recorded Books   45
Marriage Portrait, 1874   46
To a Cat Gone Blind in Its Eighteenth Summer   47
In Memory of the Nissan Stanza Wagon, 1982–1996   48

IV. FORTUNES
One by One   51
Dispatch from the Cold War, 1951   53
How Aunt Eudora Became a Post-Modern Poet   54
Leaving the Clinic   55
Deliverance   56
The Relatively Famous Poet's Mother   57
The Predator   58
Voice Mail for Wallace Stevens   59
Posthumous Instructions   60
Horace Redux   61

V. OUTSIDE THE FRAME
Outside the Frame: The Photographer's
          Last Letters to her Son   65

I. Moods

Summer Sapphics

Maybe things are better than we imagine
if a rubber inner-tube still can send us
drifting down a sinuous, tree-draped river
like the Wisconsin—

far removed from spores of *touristococcus*.
As we bob half-in and half-out of water
with our legs like tentacles, dangling limply
under the surface

we are like invertebrate creatures, floating
on a cosmic droplet—a caravan of
giant-sized amoebas, without a clear-cut
sense of direction.

It's as if we've started evolving backwards:
mammal, reptile, polliwog, protozoon—
toward that dark primordial soup we seem so
eager to get to.

Funny, how warm water will whisper secrets
in its native language to every cell— yet
we, the aggregation, have just begun to
fathom the gestures.

For Lucy, Who Came First

She simply settled down in one piece right where she was, in the
sand of a long-vanished lake edge or stream—and died.
                              —Donald C. Johanson, paleoanthropologist

When I put my hand up to my face
I can trace her heavy jawbone and the sockets
of her eyes under my skin. And in the dark
I sometimes feel her trying to uncurl
from where she sank into mudbound sleep
on that soft and temporary shore

so staggeringly long ago, time
had not yet cut its straight line
through the tangle of the planet,
nor taken up the measured sweep
that stacks the days and seasons
into an ordered past.

But I can feel her stirring
in the core of me, trying to rise up
from the deep hollow where she fell—
wanting to prowl on long callused toes
to see what made that shadow move,
to face the creature in the dark thicket

needing to know if this late-spreading dawn
will bring handfuls of berries, black
as blood, or the sting of snow,
or the steady slap of sand and weed
that wraps itself like fur
around the body.

Reading the Obituaries

Now the Barbaras have begun to die,
trailing their older sisters to the grave,
the Helens, Margies, Nans—who said goodbye
just days ago, it seems, taking their leave
a step or two behind the hooded girls
who bloomed and withered with the century—
the Dorotheas, Eleanors and Pearls
now swaying on the edge of memory.
Soon, soon, the scythe will sweep for Jeanne
and Angela, Patricia and Diane—
pause, and return for Karen and Christine
while Susan spends a sleepless night again.
Ah, Debra, how can you be growing old?
Jennifer, Michelle, your hands are cold.

Poem for a 75th Birthday

Love of my life, it's nearly evening
and here you still are, slow-dancing
in your garden, folding and unfolding
like an enormous grasshopper in the waning
sun. Somehow you've turned our rectangle
of clammy clay into Southern California,
where lilacs and morning-glories mingle
with larkspur, ladyfern and zinnia—
all of them a little drunk on thundershowers
and the broth of newly fallen flowers.

I can't get over how the brightest blooms
seem to come reaching for your hand,
weaving their way across the loom
of your fingers, bending
toward the trellis of your body.
They sway on their skinny stems
like a gang of super-models
making fabulous displays of their dumb
and utter gratitude, as if they knew
they'd be birdseed if it weren't for you.

And yet they haven't got the slightest clue
about the future; they behave as if
you'll be there for them always, as if you
were the sun itself, brilliant enough
to keep them in the pink, or gold, or green
forever. Understandable, I decide
as I look at you out there—as I lean
in your direction, absolutely satisfied
that summer afternoon is all
there is, and night will never fall.

The Blue Water Buffalo

One in 250 Cambodians, or 40,000 people,
have lost a limb to a landmine.
                    —U.N. Development Programme
                            Communications Office

On both sides of the screaming highway, the world
is made of emerald silk—sumptuous bolts of it,
stitched by threads of water into cushions
that shimmer and float on the Mekong's munificent glut.

In between them plods the ancient buffalo—dark blue
in the steamy distance, and legless
where the surface of the ditch dissects
the body from its waterlogged supports below

or it might be a woman, up to her thighs
in the lukewarm ooze, bending at the waist
with the plain grace of habit, delving for weeds
in water that receives her wrist and forearm

as she feels for the alien stalk, the foreign blade
beneath that greenest of green coverlets
where brittle pods in their corroding skins
now shift, waiting to salt the fields with horror.

The Geniuses Among Us

They take us by surprise, these tall perennials
that jut like hollyhocks above the canopy
of all the rest of us—bright testimonials
to the scale of human possibility.
They come to bloom for every generation,
blazing with extraordinary notions
from the taproots of imagination—
dazzling us with incandescent visions.
And soon, the things we never thought would happen
start to happen: the solid fences
of reality begin to soften,
crumbling into fables and romances—
and we turn away from where we've been
to a new place, where light is pouring in.

Foreigner

I have abandoned my century
and entered another that is not mine.
I am a stranger here

among hordes of graceful natives
all smooth of skin and lean of memory,
who just a day or two ago

were pounding in the sandbox with
the backs of their shovels.
In the time it's taken

to put away their diapers
they have named a new galaxy
after themselves

choreographed a tango
for silicon chip and atom,
added postmodern cantos

to civilization's epic—
while I have learned
to pick and fumble

through crumbling landmarks,
asking the way to the ruins
in the wrong language.

Notes from The Good-Girl Chronicles, 1963

I. Reminiscences of a Fly-Girl

When the friendly skies were full of virgins,
I was one of them—naive, addled,
benighted as a parakeet emerging
from its covered cage. I'd been re-modeled:
my college pleats and plaids had been replaced
by a mock-military fitted suit
and soldier-cap—utterly chaste,
yet so erotic, so forbidden-fruit,
I was the concubine inside the head
of every traveling salesman on the plane.
He'd have me stripped and bouncing into bed
with him, bearing my bottles of champagne
with giggles and conspiratorial wink—
all this before I'd poured a single drink.

II. *Porter Powell's Wife*

All this, before I'd even poured his drink:
the swift removal of his coat, a match
to light his cigarette; a moist, pale pink
lipsticky kiss; one moment more to fetch
the Wall Street Journal. Then his Crown
Royal (rocks, splash, twist), a rack of lamb,
his monologue du jour (the putting down
of one more office coup) *ad nauseam*
while I provide encouraging remarks,
followed by my mentioning the bank
and how they called today about some checks
that didn't clear. I watch his eyes go blank.
He drops his fork, rises from his place
and slaps me, hard, three times across the face.

III. Celebrity's Mother

I've slapped myself three times across the face,
so I know it's not a dream, I swear—
my babygirl has really won first place
in the beauty pageant at State Fair.
Look how she slinks on those high heels,
cranks her little hips just like a pro
down that runway—honey, she's on wheels,
she's headed for the Johnny Carson show.
Come on, sweetheart, talk a little louder,
bat those lashes, lick your lips a lot;
make your poor old mama even prouder—
grab for what your mama never got.
Thank you, Jesus! Thank you, Maidenform!
Just watch my baby take the world by storm.

IV. Sixteen

I didn't want to take the world by storm—
just hoped to be a wife and mom someday,
but I've blown it all to kingdom come
because this boy and I went all the way.
I can't imagine what got into me
(except for him, of course) because I'm smart,
I know how boys will hold you close and cry
and make up stories that you take to heart
before they drop you like a shoe—and smirk
at you for buying into all their shit.
I guess I'm just another dirty joke,
a stupid nympho they can laugh about.
I never was a bargain anyhow,
but nobody would ever want me now.

V. George and Vera Carter's Wonderful Daughter

Nobody will ever want me more
than my sullen, shrinking parents do;
they think the very fact that I was born
proves I owe them both a thing or two.
So I've become the daughter that they crave—
a loyal and obedient retainer
who brings them what they need to stay alive
and well—from laxatives to Sunday dinner.
I listen to them re-arrange the past
to suit themselves (their favorite diversion)
and see to it they fall asleep at last,
allowing me an evening for submersion
in that alarming book I bought last week:
something called *The Feminine Mystique*.

VI. *The Block-Watcher*

You could call it a feminine mistake,
that thing my neighbor did—her moving out
like that. At night! She didn't even take
her clothes; just her hat and overcoat,
some books, and boom!—she's out the door.
Just drove away without a word to Bob—
because she knew he meant it when he swore
that he would *never* let her get a job.
I guess she thinks her fancy education
entitles her to some sort of "career",
like that bunch from Women's Liberation
who bellyache and burn their underwear.
But if you ask me, she's acting like a brat,
throwing away her happiness like that.

VII. Mrs. McKinney Looks Back

I've thrown away my happiness, like that
old crone in the fairy tale. I'm frail
and shriveled now—and haunted by the thought
of what I might have been, had I been male:
I'd probably have taken center stage
in some exciting, world-altering dance.
But it's been such a stupefying age
for women. No one cared whether we flounced
or crawled through all the tragicomic phases
of our lives—we nearly always played
our grand theatricals to empty houses.
But I can't blame the men. They understood
the world was theirs, with all of its diversions—
just look: the skies are filled with friendly virgins!

II. States of Mind

Subject to Change

—A reflection on my students

They are so beautiful, and so very young
they seem almost to glitter with perfection,
these creatures that I briefly move among.

I never get to stay with them for long,
but even so, I view them with affection:
they are so beautiful, and so very young.

Poised or clumsy, placid or high-strung,
they're expert in the art of introspection,
these creatures that I briefly move among—

And if their words don't quite trip off the tongue
consistently, with just the right inflection,
they remain beautiful. And very young.

Still, I have to tell myself it's wrong
to think of them as anything but fiction,
these creatures that I briefly move among—

Because, like me, they're traveling headlong
in that familiar, vertical direction
that coarsens *beautiful*, blackmails *young*,
and turns to phantoms those I move among.

On Learning, Late in Life, that
Your Mother Was a Jew

Methuselah something. Somethingsomething Ezekiel.
—Albert Goldbarth

So that explains it, you say to yourself.
And for one split second, you confront
the mirror like a Gestapo operative—
narrow-eyed, looking for the telltale hint,

the giveaway (jawline, profile, eyebrow)—
something visible that could account
for this, the veritable key
to your life story and its denouement.

It seems the script that you were handed
long ago, with all its blue-eyed implications,
can now be seen as something less than candid—
a laundry list of whoppers and omissions.

It's time for something else to float
back in from theology's deep end: the strains,
perhaps, of *A-don o-lam,* drowning out
the peals of *Jesus the Conqueror Reigns,*

inundating the lily and the rose,
stifling the saints (whose dogged piety
never did come close, God knows,
to causing many ripples of anxiety)

and you're waiting for the revelation
on its way this minute, probably—

the grand prelude to your divine conversion,
backlit with ritual and pageantry.

But nothing happens. Not a thing. No song,
no *shofar,* no compelling Shabbat call
to prayer—no signal that your heart belongs
to David, rather than your old familiar, Paul.

Where does a faithless virgin go from here,
after being compromised by two
competing testimonies to thin air—
when both of them are absolutely true?

I Miss You and I'm Drunk

Look at the way the moon just sits there
with its brights on, aiming
that yellowish beam across the water
at the lovers and the skinnydippers

and how the summer sawgrass
grabs me by the ankles, making me
stumble, making me think about
the flaming ache of falling down on top of you

and how you would cup my face
between your hands and stare at me
crosseyed—God knows what you saw there
but it was always enough

to start us banging together like
a couple of drunk drivers—woozy,
reckless through the barricades, catching
fire, turning over and over

till we finally hit the ground
smoking, practically unconscious
with the moon all over us.
And that is why I plan

to spend the night right here
on this besotted beach—to carve
another tire-track in the sand, deep
and warped with complications.

The Belgian Half

Listen, I don't have a grandmother
on that side, never did. Never knew
any bantamweight woman in black kid shoes
stirring blancmange in a darkening kitchen,
ceiling adrip with anise-scented steam.

Couldn't tell you if she cried when her only son
bolted for New York, sleek little man
with narrow feet, ascot, nostrils on the move—
don't know if she heard about his plan to marry,
which he did (skinny lady in an ermine coat)

Or that he'd fathered a child—
so I've no idea if there might have been
grief in that kitchen or a wrinkled hand to hold,
to comfort in its coldest hour, with *Viens, viens,
Grand-maman—I am the daughter of your boy.*

The Aging Huntress Speaks to Her Reflection

Dear old moon of a face,
you've been looking back at me
for decades now

always giving me your best tilt
and a little quiver of lies—
but don't I love you for it?

Don't I fix my gaze on all
your nubbins and craters,
know your geography by heart?

Maybe I'll take you to town tonight,
tricked out in gilt and camouflage—
see how it goes with the men.

Not the young ones, those cheerful bucks
who look at you with all their teeth
thinking: *Teapot. Hairpin. Marianne Moore.*

It's their fathers, beery and balding—
and the loners in their silver ponytails,
heartbreakingly wistful—

they're the ones I want
to cool my heels with, feel
the warm breath of on my neck

while we knock a few back,
shoot the breeze, bathe together
in your fading borrowed light.

Always Questions

Yesterday? At the mall? I bought
a book of Emily Dickinson
for my mom?
                    —overheard at Hardee's

There is a moment, in the middle teens,
when virtually every sentence ends
on an upward curl, as if it really means
to be a question—or at least pretends

to entertain an element of doubt—
like this: *I started early? Took my dog ?*
suggesting that I may have ventured out
exceptionally *late*, to take a jog

without the dog, or anyone else, along.
And if I add: *and visited the sea?*
I'm hinting that of course I could be wrong
about this *sea* thing, ha-ha, you know me.

It's evidently hard for them to say
the thing they mean, without a little cue
for feedback, for the understood *Okay*;
or, possibly, they talk the way they do

because they are the representatives
of a long-out-of-date civility—
these gentle souls who speak in tentatives,
and choose to dwell in possibility.

Explication of a True Story

For Lani, my college roommate

Now that you've told me
what my father did to you
in the boat on Lake Mendota
the summer we both turned twenty—
that there had been a moment when he
carefully released his grip
from the throttle of the Evinrude
and snaked his hand down inside
the top of your magenta bathing suit—
     I understand *the plot.*

And when I think about your face,
your startled rage, your fierce blush,
I recall that your assaulter was a man
who went about his everyday affairs
a scion of respectability, genteel
down to his cordovans: the linen
handkerchief, the perfect press
in his Van Heusen shirt, the *ching*
of change in a front pocket—
     These are the *symbolic elements.*

I did see him naked once,
when I was nine. He lay sprawled
across his bed, snoring like a diesel
in the slatted sunlight.
Between his legs lay coiled his
enormous apparatus—a gilded pile
of gunnery which even then I sensed

26

boded mighty ill for somebody, sometime.
This you would call *foreshadowing*.

And I'm sure that every thought
you have of me dissolves into that day
on the lake. You have it memorized
by now, and I am always at the heart of it:
the other one violated—the daughter, mortified.
That would be the *moral* of the story.
The *message*. The *denouement*.

Legacy

Jake is six years old, and he has learned
that long ago his grandpa was a soldier
in the Good War (that's what Grandpa calls it),
the finest war this country ever had.
And every night before he falls asleep
Jake can almost hear his grandpa clattering
through the woods on that bum leg of his,
stomping up and down a German hillside—
nearly sees him in the smoky distance,
his threadbare skull glinting like a helmet
through the round hole in his hair;
and he would almost certainly be singing
Praise the Lord and Pass the Ammunition—
a song that never fails to agitate
the dusky underbrush of almost-sleep
when the two of them are holding hands,
waiting for the great and glorious morning
when all the other grandpas in the outfit—
waving their canes and singing *We are all
between perdition and the deep blue sea*
finally find them, finally come rumbling
up the driveway in their golden tanks.

After Twenty Years

A dangerous business, Mother,
leaving your memory solely in my care—
I've always been incompetent
in matters memorial and monumental,
and I can't hold onto you much longer.

You have faded to a sepia glimmer
in my head, and I'm having trouble
retrieving you from my gallery of still-lifes.
Even your quaint name, *Alice,* melts
to nearly nothing on my tongue.

But if I should be driving past a row
of brick-and-shingle bungalows
when maple leaves are sticking to the sidewalk
and a rain-glossed school bus starts to swing
its yellow bulk around the corner,

there you are again—framed in a wavy
leaded window, watering a long-fingered
philodendron while the Victrola
clatters out Landowska's version of
the *Little Preludes* through the glass

and I am nine years old—and you,
the center of my small universe,
are the love of my life, to whose powdered
presence I come home blissfully,
day after dangerous day

utterly innocent of a distant time
when you will turn from me

and withdraw into my archive of losses,
where the rising dust will dim,
then darken, and then obliterate.

Women at Sixty

turn from their bodies
in embarrassment, as if
they had found themselves
wearing the wrong thing.
They wonder how
it could have come to this,
how the gardenia flesh
could have wilted on the stem,
and how the boys they married
could be hovering like mayflies
around the wet-bar, learning
the slow idioms of old men.

They try to bring to mind
what they were doing
on the day growing old began:
opting for the condominium,
the artificial Christmas tree?
Catching their children speaking
in profundities? Or was it when
they first noticed, thunderstruck,
that their fickle bodies were
casually betraying them—
relentlessly eroding under
the damask of their skin?

It no longer takes them
by surprise, this revelation.
They have begun to understand
that they (of all people)
must finally slip into the role
of *elder*, of *relic*, of *crone*

and take their leave—gathering
their cloaks about them,
holding the edges tightly
at the throat.

Rondeau: Old Woman With Cat

Osteoporosis (one of life's indignities)
is such a splendid name for the disease—
all those little o's, holes in the bone
where the rain gets in, rendering a crone
like me defective, porous as swiss cheese.

I'm riddled at the hips and knees,
roundsided as parentheses
since my shrunken spine has known
    osteoporosis—

and my extremities
have shriveled into lacy filigrees,
breakable as glass on stone.
Naked at the window ledge I drone
to my sleek, supple Siamese:
    osteoporosis.

Father Goose

Mel, Mel, the Dad from Hell
Raised your kids in a padded cell—
Not one soul cried the night you died,
But Mother giggled like a bride.

III. Scenes

Aunt Eudora's Harlequin Romance

She turns the bedlamp on. The book falls open
in her mottled hands, and while she reads
her mouth begins to quiver, forming words
like *Breathless. Promises. Elope.*
As she turns the leaves, Eudora's cheek
takes on a bit of bloom. Her frowzy hair
thickens and turns gold, her dim eyes clear,
the wattles vanish from her slender neck.
Her waist, emerging from its ring of flesh,
bends to the side. Breasts that used to hang
like pockets rise and ripen; her long legs
tremble. Her eyes close, she holds her breath—
the steamy pages flutter by, unread,
as lover after lover finds her bed.

Another Thing I Ought to Be Doing

So now I should be taking special care
of them, is that it? Every month go pat
pat pat—when what they've done for me is flat
out bloody nothing? Case in point: where
were they when I was fourteen, fifteen,
and topographically a putting green?

Not to mention nights when I disgraced
my gender, stuffing tissue paper down
my polo shirt or confirmation gown—
my philosophy on staying chaste
having less to do with things profound
than fear of giving off a crunchy sound.

And now you're saying, *Minister to them!*
these very breasts that caused me great gymnasiums
of misery and high humiliation—
Institute a monthly regimen!
meaning I'm to walk my fingers gingerly
around these two molehills in front of me.

Sorry, but my hands have dropped straight down
like baby birds. They will not rise
to the occasion, won't get organized,
refuse to land on enemy terrain.
They simply twitch and fidget in my lap
as if they sense a booby trap—

As if they hear the moron in my head
insisting that I'll never be caught dead.

The Native

In Tokyo, or maybe Nagasaki,
you'll find a photo of Yours Truly, taken
down at Wolski's Tavern in Milwaukee,
early in the Ford administration.

I was wearing short-shorts, and a cotton
T-shirt (tie-dyed pink, running to green),
plus a sweater—carefully flea-bitten
in the manner favored by James Dean.

A chartered bus was idling right behind me
as tourists from Japan leapt out the door,
their flashbulbs blasting bright enough to blind me,
preserving me on film forevermore.

And now, years later, when they wax nostalgic
about their thrilling trip to the U.S.,
they'll peer and gape again at that authentic
outback woman, in her native dress.

.

Splitting

Higgledy-piggledy
Ernest Lord Rutherford
Showed how uranium
Tends to decay

Just like a love affair:
Radioactively
Or in some other com-
Bustible way.

Inventing the Love Poets

I think I see her crouching, pen in hand
on an old dilapidated mattress,
a lock of moonlit hair coming unpinned
as she writes, achingly, about her losses

while he, entangled in designer sheets,
enters my head buck-naked, gloomily
scrawling debaucheries about deceit
while swigging from a pint of J & B.

Don't want to hear that he's an overweight
associate professor who takes bran
for breakfast—or that she's the ultimate
suburban mom, with dog and minivan—

I'm so enraptured by their sweet effusions,
I'll stick (thanks anyway) to my illusions.

Aunt Eudora in Paris

Somewhere in this vast and graceful city
there stands a little café *venerable;*
Eudora finds its tiles and sideboards pretty
and seats herself behind a tiny *table.*

Thinking it an admirable venue
for practicing her skills in *la français,*
Eudora spreads before herself a menu—
LaRousse a handy finger-lick away.

A waiter, expert in the art of sneering
creatively, the way Parisians do,
addresses her while fingering his earring:
Madame, we have no hamburgers for you.

Eudora lifts one eyebrow, pats her hair,
and with a queenly, autocratic look
says: *Vas faire foutre a la vache, monsieur!*
and turns again, serenely, to her book.

And that, *mon petit chou*, is why Eudora
is grinning like a gargoyle as she sits
wondering how to break it to her lawyer
she's leaving every penny to Berlitz.

The Adulterer's Waltz

Look at me, sitting here sniffing and dabbing my eyes
with a hanky, because you are going away. Pathetic,
wouldn't you say? I rehearsed this particular pose
in the mirror for days: nothing melodramatic,
I said to myself. Just a touch of the innocent martyr,
a tiny suggestion of injury—biting the lip,
for example, rather than staging one of those rip-snorter
tantrums, the kind your wife will use to trap
you, and send you slithering back to the suburb from whence
you came, where your silver Mercedes still resides,
and where you can keep the pleat in your gabardine pants
as you recollect this asinine masquerade
that ends tonight. Go away, go away, and take
your Wordsworth with you. I've got a phone call to make.

Surveying the Damage

Bailey's Harbor, March 2001

Even after catastrophes like this one,
I've heard it can be done—

that the damp hearth of the senses
can be poked and stirred

until the embers, still breathing
after an old fire, manage a feeble wink

and the low clouds might be at last contained
behind slant pickets of daylight

and the sky patched into something
nearing blue again—spliced, at least,

by a passing osprey riding a downdraft
all the way from the Apostles

just as a storm-door, rattling its hinges
against the late debacle, opens wide

onto a shoreline paved with residual snow,
gleaming like a coral reef.

Listening to Recorded Books

In this dominion
of aural delights
I reclaim the child I was,
the one who snacked
on the plummy spells
of Milne and Stevenson,
Lewis and Lear

and I receive
what I'm fed—
swallow and wait
for the next mellifluous
spoonful of Dickens,
Defoe, Cather, Fitzgerald,
or Henry James
in aspic.

I'm a queen bee, a goose
in a box, a debauchee—not
of dew, but DuMaurier—
licking my lips over
audible savories,
fattening up on a rich
confiture of words.

Marriage Portrait, 1874

Did they ever laugh, these two solemn creatures?
Smirk into their collars, or liberate
a short guffaw at Evensong?

And mornings when the sermon seemed
especially absurd, did tears of hilarity
glaze their quivering cheeks?

Did he dare press his palm against her
kneeling thigh? Might she, mouthing the *Doxology*,
have nudged him with the toe of her shoe?

How long would it have taken him to unbutton
a shoe like that, undo her Sunday gown?
Did they ever run all the way home?

To a Cat Gone Blind in Its 18th Summer

Every time you come back home to us
from one of your dazzling Imax dreams,
a map of the known world unrolls
under the touchpads of your feet,
where shaggy broadloom prairie
gives way to the slick hinterlands
of linoleum and wooden floor.

You've returned to the great indoors,
a finite universe where cacophony
draws back: snarling Airedale is reduced
to sputtering fool, the power mower
rendered meek and harmless.
Even your fellow cats seem irrelevant,
being clearly otherwise engaged.

At the high window, a sparrow
is fretting. Your gaze swivels
smoothly in his direction and beyond,
as if you saw not only him, but also
his vestigial shadow (mercurial
in your mind's almond eye)
crossing a field of preposterous green
where it's April again and again.

In Memory of the Nissan Stanza Wagon, 1982–1996

You hardly ever see one nowadays—
they're nearly gone. Endangered, anyhow,
because of the intensifying craze
for S.U.V.s, the industry's cash cow—

but some of us remember how it felt
to climb into that barren, boxy space,
yank and snap the fraying safety belt
and dream of glitz, and speed, and careless grace—

all the things our Stanzas never had
by any stretch. But as we chugged
year after year along the same old road,
(handicapped, some said, by what we dragged

behind us from an unenlightened time),
we could sense a subtle turnabout:
our Stanzas were acquiring some acclaim
in circles with considerable clout.

Perhaps it was because we knew our beat
so well, the basic letter of the law,
while improvising several ways to cheat
a little, cut some corners, raise the bar

on all the disagreements, groans and whines
about what Stanzas could or couldn't do.
So if one comes your way, check out the lines
and brakes. Make it yours. And make it new.

IV. Fortunes

One by One

Now You are closing down my five senses, slowly,
and I am an old man lying in darkness.
　　　　　　　　　　　　　　　—Czeslaw Milosz

First, I will draw backward from the stench
of living; I will make myself immune
to its erotic sweats and stinks, quench
my lust for one more August afternoon,
the steam of which will be forgotten soon—
the human brain is that incompetent
at conjuring the memory of scent.

Then I will put my fingers to my ears
to silence the brass bands performing there
with frills and flourishes, greeting the years
as they sweep past. Instead, I will prepare
a quiet room for taking in the spare
continuo of leaves dropping from trees—
no harmonies are more profound than these.

The trick is to un-feel what one has felt
against the fingertip, the cheek, the groin—
that rare capacity we all were dealt
for knowing lavish pleasures, rattling pain,
lethal implosions where the two conjoin.
I un-remember them, I dis-evoke,
I let them dwindle into air and smoke.

Foreground, background. Particle and field.
Every law that proves or justifies
the separateness of things has been repealed:
contours and edges melt before my eyes

and there is nothing left to recognize.
Blinking, I sit behind a watery scrim,
watching forms and colors seep and swim.

Now I will push aside the bedside glass
of medicated liquor, thick and sour,
refuse to let its chalk and brimstone pass
over my tongue. I yield, at this late hour,
to the obliteration of my power,
relinquish my compulsion to consume.
My shadow curls. I am the one consumed.

Dispatch from the Cold War, 1951

On New Years Eve, my father force-fed lumps
of anthracite into the gap-toothed mouth
of the old furnace—I heard the manic thump
of his shovel on the grate. Its thick breath
stammered, then roared against the damp
basement walls, where smells of ancient earth
gave a pagan edge to his attempt
to conjure fire with concentrated wrath.

Soon he sent a clot of hot air seeping
up the stairs, through ducts and vestibules
to the attic window-frames and rafters,
scorching the chimney-pots before escaping
to the starlit sky. The house went cold;
my father left for good shortly thereafter.

How Aunt Eudora Became
a Post-Modern Poet

A girl is not supposed to write that way
(the teachers told her in the seventh grade)—
you ought to find more proper things to say.

For instance, there's no reason to portray
your daddy sucking gin like lemonade—
young girls are not supposed to write that way.

And we don't care to read an exposé
on how your mama gets the grocer paid;
there have to be more proper things to say.

Why not write about a nice bouquet
of flowers, or a waterfall, instead?
You cannot be allowed to write the way

you did, for instance, when your Uncle Ray
was entertaining strangers in his bed,
and what the county sheriff had to say.

Why must you put these matters on display?
You're going to regret it, I'm afraid—
remember, you're a girl. So *write* that way.
Go find yourself some proper things to say.

Leaving the Clinic

Baja California, 1997

Having carried your own
terrible frailness
to the edge of the water

you bent your body sharply
like a broken stick, until
you were kneeling in the sand.

*If the world weren't so damned
beautiful,* you said, *maybe
dying wouldn't be so bad—*

But then you saw how a small rain
had pocked the creamy skin
of the beach overnight

causing snails to leave their sanctuaries,
and the pursed hibiscus buds
to fatten and explode,

and with the sea collapsing around us,
thinning to a glassy sheen
that blinded you

you hid your face
behind your hands and shook
with unrequited love.

Deliverance

Talbot Island, Florida

Felled by a wind-shear deadly as Vesuvius,
three adolescent live-oak trees have spread
their naked bodies on the beach—oblivious
to the explicit fact that they are dead.

Maintaining the accoutrements of "tree"
they sprawl across the sand, immobilized—
three topknots floating in the shallow sea,
three clumps of frizzy pubic roots, exposed.

Sun-bleached to marble whiteness, they could pass
for Grecian statues, fallen but intact,
still clinging to the crumbling godliness
we give to every ancient artifact.

But they are merely trees—not Hera's daughters
fixed in stone or glorified in myth—
still, their pathetic fall seems all that matters
here, where we confront their early death.

Unnerved, we peer beyond this spread of sand
and out to sea, mile after watery mile—
shading our vision with a helpless hand,
ignoring the horizon's long, thin smile.

The Relatively Famous Poet's Mother

She will be thick
of thigh and torso, noticeably dense
upstairs, and yet phenomenally quick
to view a certain person's eloquence
as lunatic.

Her ample breast
will of gardenias and/or garlic reek;
and (oddly, for a creature so repressed)
she'll see to it that someone gets a peek
at her undressed.

She will not care
for poetry, considering it strange
and deviant, if not downright bizarre—
and she suspects that poets seldom change
their underwear.

It's no surprise
that her uncharitable attitude
seems so disgraceful in the poet's eyes
that there will be no poems of gratitude
until she dies.

And even then,
the poet—stricken, sniffling in despair,
might scrawl a line or two with doubtful pen—
then shred it all to ribbons, saying *there
she goes again.*

The Predator

In the neglected gardens of the long-married,
a small brown owl is sleeping, has been sleeping
since the days when the petals fell from most
of the roses. It has settled into in the dark
and damp, under sheets of ancient silt.

It has been known to stir in the presence
of notes from a song it has heard
before, amplified on a high wind—
or a name that flutters up
unbidden, creating in its wake a surge of yearning.

But should there come an imminence
of mouth or tongue, it flings itself awake:
eyes widening, claws extending, curling around
the hard black seeds of deceit. From deep
in the genes, it lays its brutal plans.

Voice Mail for Wallace Stevens

Wallace—(did they really call you *Wallace*?)
I'd like a word with you, now that you've got
your lock on immortality: you wrote
in euphonies, making the angels jealous,
then went ahead and dared the rest of us
to deconstruct the textual implications.
Well—about a million dissertations
later—there's still no consensus, Wallace.
Just incessant inharmoniousness
along with thirteen thousand ways of looking
at a bird, a nightgown, or the plucking
of a strange guitar. In fact, I guess
we'll never chase your tigers very far,
nor trap your perfect genius in a jar.

Posthumous Instructions

After the fire, when I am rattling in my urn
and have no more to say to you, go home.
Have lunch. Ignore me, while I try to learn
the etiquette of ash and clinkerdom.

Let me settle. Let me reconcile
my boundaries with the cold geometry
of this strange vessel—my new domicile
whose curving contours reconfigure me.

Let me liberate the elements
that fused in me the morning I was formed
and offer them again, as evidence
that my short visit left the world unharmed.

My severance is what the world regains:
you do not need to scatter my remains.

Horace Redux

Hold it right there, my superstitious friend—
Don't waste your money on the zodiac
Or sell the farm to some religious quack
To find out when your life is going to end.

It's obvious we're not supposed to know
If we've got one more winter left, or oodles.
So dry the dishes, go and walk the poodles—
The odds are good you'll live to see it snow.

And even if the surface of the lake
Should freeze (the way it did when we were boys),
Observing it from here or from the skies
Makes not a shred of difference to the lake.

So pour yourself another glass of port
Before your dithering becomes addictive—
Then smile, drink up, and keep Time in perspective
If it kills you, buddy. Life is short.

V. Outside the Frame

Outside the Frame:
The Photographer's Last Letters to her Son

I.

Wildwood Farm, April 3rd

Dear Chipper,
      Well, it's starting over—April's
back debauching us again, the woods
are soaking wet, the mud dazzles, all
our stringy willow trees are going blond
and sentimental (just like the women
who write about them)—and I rise to the sight
of the grass nudging up green, brimming
with narcissi, practically overnight!
—Narcissi. From a distance, don't they look
like froth? Or whitecaps? Makes me want to run
away to sea—*my* sea, Chip. A maverick
ocean that doesn't move, but invites me in
to take its photograph, to document
its miracles. So this morning, in I went. . .

April 20th

It's my seventy-fifth April (sixty-fourth
with a camera in my hand). . .and you wonder
why I desert my comfortable hearth
to crouch down on a patch of soggy tundra
taking pictures in the cold. Well, I'll
tell you why: it's to press my hands

against that rough young grass, to feel it yield
under my fingers, then to turn my lens
on the wetness underneath, where the soil
hides its buried treasure. Granite pearls,
flint sequins, limestone underpinnings—they're all
uncovered now, everything's exposed! The voyeur
in me goes feverish inside my head
watching seeds moving in their satin bed.

April 29th

. . .I'm cold today, Chipper. My jeans have two
black ovals in front from where I knelt
to watch the moss, and it was well past noon
before I gave it up. (Everyone thought
I'd stayed too long; guess I'm getting old
and strange. . .) But where was I? Mice? No, moss.
The farmers used to call it "elfin gold"
because it only grows in crevices
and caves. It doesn't want the sun at all—
just what the sun leaves behind, the dwindling
evidence of light—something like the pall
that hovers around a burnt-out candle.
They found me humming, reading with my thumb
its little poem to the millennium. . .

II .

Massachusetts General Hospital, May 22nd

In response to your rude questions
on the state of my health: I am of sound mind

and in my hands I hold the weight
of my soul, a leaden comfort

in my palm. Its polished crystal eye
opens, finds, fixes on the edges

of the enemy: a wall of grass,
leaves, stems and stalks, tangles

of roots and vines—the wild green Other
that follows me, no matter how

I slash and scythe my little path—
pursues me, even as I back away.

III.

Roundtree Convalescent Home,   October 2

I must compose
myself, Chipper
and admit to you
that I am terribly
frightened, the camera
has developed so many
numbers and dials
I forget what the
mean; its rings
and buttons are all
mixed up and when
I finally try
to take a shot all
I see is parts
of my own eye
bristling with
daggers, staring
back at me
grotesque and huge

I must compose
and focus the lens
for precise pinpoint
focusing I must turn
the focusing ring until
the shimmering image
becomes sharp I must
use fast shutter speeds
to stop action stop
action or I will produce
a deliberate blur except
for certain unusual
lighting situations when
I must use the exposure
compensation dial to prevent
over-exposure I must
turn and turn until
the split image
becomes whole.

IV.

Wildwood Farm, January 25

Obviously the FBI
has come to find hard
evidence of my
incompetence. They
think they're fooling me,
they even say I
have met them before,
but I have never
met them before, these
blond harpies who keep
asking me my name
and what day it is
today (Up yours-day?)
and the exact where-
abouts of my gloves
and earmuffs,
the pinking shears,
the keys to the
boathouse, my Knirps
umbrella (as if I
needed one in winter!),
the pancake syrup,
the bottle of
cocktail onions,
the thumbtacks, the
remote control
TV channel changer,
extra extra pink
Pepto-Bismol,
some kitchen

safety matches
and a couple
of bowls of excellent
vanilla custard
from Christmas.

V.

. . .whereas now I hold my hands
at arm's length and point
my index fingers skyward
and extend my thumbs
so that they meet tip to tip
thus making a frame (minus the top)

and with my frame I scan
the scenery; here a clump
of white buildings,
there a face, or a flower,
but so often nothing, Chip—
nothing at all

VI.

The loud-talking
women are back
with their folding

table and their
jigsaw puzzle:
"A Yorkshire Dale"

showing part of
a hill and some
trees with huge holes

in them as if
a cannonball
had torn through their

upper reaches.
Try, the women
yell, to find the

pieces, look, here
is some sky! But
it's hard, because

many are lost,
some are under
the table or

buried in the
cushions, a few
have been purloined—

slipped into the
untied bathrobe
of a hairless

geezer who says
he knows just where
the big tower

went. Meanwhile in
our ears someone
croons *Would we like*

to swing on a
star? and at last
they wheel away

the puzzle and
bring another
in, dumping it

out and smiling—
as if to say
Maybe you won

that round, grandmaw,
but it's just a
matter of time.

VII.

All I know is that it's
about this big and I need it for
the things I do but
I can't remember
what it's called. You put it
in the bigger thing
and it keeps it there
for you so when you want
to look at something later
there it is.
You know what I mean,
it's about so big
and it's not square,
it isn't square at all,
it's that other.
You have to use it
to make things stay where
they used to be
so you can take them out
and look at them where they were.
But God help me I
can't find it anywhere.
All I know for certain
is that it's about this big
and I need it, I need it very much.

VIII.

Have you come to say hello
maybe you will take me
I think it must be time
time to go now
goodbye

IX.

There are times each day
     when I go   off
                  somewhere

when I return there is a little less of me
     as if
     each time

              mind and
        one thread of memory

           were pulled away

     become
Soon I shall be
     entirely
      unravelled

I shall survive
     as
       afterimage
     as
       gatherer of light

Marilyn L. Taylor, who teaches at the University of Wisconsin at Milwaukee, has been named Poet Laureate of the city of Milwaukee for 2004-2005. Her work has been published in a number of journals and anthologies, including *The American Scholar, Iris, The Formalist*, and *Poetry Magazine's 90th Anniversary Anthology*. Winner of the 2003 Dogwood Prize, she also took first place in recent competitions sponsored by *Passager, The Ledge, GSU Review,* and won the Anamnesis Press Award for her chapbook, *Exit Only*. Other awards include a Wisconsin Arts Board fellowship and an "Intro" Award from AWP.

Printed in the United States
76690LV00002B/1-99